She tells them construction is, "Just so much fun."
"And you have something great,
when you are all done."

Her friends are now curious
and want to know more.
So she takes them right down,
to the best hardware store.

Connie's mom and dad join them all for the trip.
To look at the pliers and wrenches and clips.

Once they arrive, Connie rushes inside.
Puts her hands on her hips
and stares with wide eyes.

She shows off the ladders,
the hammers, the saws.
And the bins full of bolts and nails,
right by the door.

She points out the gloves,
safety glasses and files.
They look at each shelf
and examine each aisle.

Then she walks them out back
and what do they see.
A sight that makes Connie dizzy with glee.

There, parked before them,
are trucks of all kinds.
And "Safety First" written on big orange signs.

Bulldozers and dump trucks,
cement mixers and more.
Excavators and cranes,
turn on engines and roar.

Connie and her friends,
all clap and scream.
When right there before them,
is a construction team.

The workers get ready,
grab tools and their gear.
They wave to the kids and then she appears.

One construction worker
walks up to the crew.
She looks right at Connie
and Connie just knew.

It was a woman, with a hardhat and key.
Just what little Connie, someday wished to be.

She asks Connie's parents
if the kids want to see.
The inside of the trucks
and they all agree.

Connie is first and hops up inside.
She is ready for a wild construction crew ride.

She tries all the levers, buttons and gears.
Moves the big scoop in front,
without even a fear.

She gets to see tools, so many in fact.
The woman says,
"This one you don't have to give back."

She gives Connie a tape measure
and then walks away.
It's the one Connie uses,
to this very day.

She brings it to use on her construction sites.
When she builds skyscrapers
that soar to great heights.

Connie knew she could do it, she truly did.
Even when she was a curious,
creative young kid.

Anyone can do it, whatever you like.
Cooking, construction or building cool bikes.

Just believe in yourself
and follow your dreams.
Even if they are made up of
hammers and beams.

Make something wonderful, whatever you do.
Stay true to your passion and stay true to you.

THE END